FROM THE FILMS OF

Harry Potter™

AROUND THE WIZARDING WORLD
ACTIVITY BOOK

W9-AZU-491

WIZARDING WORLD

SCHOLASTIC INC.

ISBN 978-1-338-82304-2

10 9 8 7 6 5 4 3 2 1   22 23 24 25 26
Printed in Malaysia   106

First edition 2022

By Jasper Meadowsweet
Book design by Becky James and Jessica Meltzer
Additional illustrations by Violet Tobacco
Stock photos © Shutterstock.com

In your hands is a very special book. By using the foil paper, you'll be able to decorate scenes and images with shiny colors.

1

Select the color of foil paper that you'd like to use. Set aside.

2

In the pages of the book, carefully peel the area that you'd like to color with foil. (Note: It should already be perforated.) Discard the peeled top.

3

Pick up the foil paper you set aside in step 1. With the color side facing you, press the foil paper into the area of the page that you just peeled.

Tip: You should see the outline of the shape that you're decorating through the foil sheet.

4

Slowly peel the sheet of foil away. Ta-da! Admire your creation.

Tip: Once you've used a section of foil, it cannot be reused. We recommend starting with a corner of the sheet when decorating to maximize your foil paper.

SORTING CEREMONY

Students at Hogwarts are sorted into their houses by wearing the Sorting Hat. The Sorting Hat peers into the minds of the young witches and wizards to best determine where they belong.

When the Sorting Hat placed Harry in Gryffindor, it also considered putting him in Slytherin. Where would you have placed Harry if you could choose? Use your foil to show what you decide!

 BLUE: RAVENCLAW

 SCARLET: GRYFFINDOR

 GREEN: SLYTHERIN

 YELLOW: HUFFLEPUFF

Harry was sorted into Gryffindor, which is for the brave, courageous, and determined. But there are brave, courageous, and determined members of other houses too — Luna Lovegood is a Ravenclaw through and through (she's witty and creative), and she also charges into battle at the drop of a quill!

If you could choose a Hogwarts house for yourself, what would it be and why? Write your answer below!

RAVenClAw because I hAve a good mind

QUIDDITCH PITCH

Quidditch is a popular sport at Hogwarts that's played on broomsticks. There are seven players per team: two Beaters, one Keeper, three Chasers, and a Seeker.

Using your foil colors, decorate the scene below. What colors are the seats around the Quidditch pitch? Can you spot the Golden Snitch? (Hint: You may want to use gold foil to decorate it!)

Think about a sport that you
play or would like to play. What makes
it so fun? Write your answer below!

Football
because I like
catching a ball

POTIONS CLASS

Professor Snape teaches Potions during Harry's first year at Hogwarts. There are lots and lots of potions that witches and wizards can brew—and they're all different colors, such as the gold Felix Felicis (liquid luck) and Polyjuice Potion, which changes colors based on the person the drinker is trying to transform into.

Felix Felicis

Poor Hermione learns just how powerful the Polyjuice Potion is in her second year — she accidentally turns herself into a cat!

What color potion is Hermione brewing? Color it in!

POLYJUICE POTION

Another kind of potion is Amortentia, a love potion. Whoever drinks Amortentia falls in love with the person who brewed it. But of course, real love can't be bottled. As soon as the potion wears off, so too do their lovesick feelings.

Think about someone you love. Then draw them in the frame on the next page.

Did you know? Amortentia smells different to every person. That's because the love potion smells like their favorite thing.

What would your Amortentia smell like? Write your answer below!

_____

_____

_____

_____

_____

_____

_____

_____

_____

_____

LOVE POTION

Now imagine that you are helping Hermione brew a potion! You get to foil, design, and decorate it yourself. What color is your potion? What about the bubbles coming from the cauldron?

Don't forget to choose your potion ingredients too! Circle the ones you would use in the list below.

Fluxweed (Ginger Root)

Boomslang Skin

(Lacewing Flies) (Honey)

Eye of Newt   Troll Bogeys

Dandelion Root

Acromantula Venom

(Wolfsbane)

DIAGON ALLEY

Harry is introduced to Diagon Alley by Hagrid just before Harry begins his first year at Hogwarts. Diagon Alley is a cobblestoned shopping area where magical folk go to buy wands, robes, and so much more.

It is in Diagon Alley that Hagrid buys
Hedwig for Harry's birthday. If you could
have any animal companion, what would it be?
Why? Write your answer below!

a wolf because
It is close
to a dog, but
more fieke!

GRINGOTTS WIZARDING BANK

One popular destination in Diagon Alley is Gringotts Wizarding Bank. Wizards and witches visit the bank to deposit or withdraw valuable items in Gringotts' vaults, including jewelry, family heirlooms, and money. Wizarding money is made up of coins—bronze Knuts, silver Sickles, and gold Galleons.

Using your foil, decorate this vault! What color are the shiny stones? What about the stacks of coins?

Gringotts is one of the safest places in the wizarding world. Like Hagrid told Harry in the first film, "Ain't no place safer, 'cept perhaps Hogwarts."

Can you spot the hidden Sorcerer's Stone on this page?

OLLIVANDERS

Also located in Diagon Alley is Ollivanders wand shop. Mr. Ollivander and his family have been making wands since 382 B.C.E. Mr. Ollivander can remember every wand he ever sold.

Using your foil colors, decorate the wand shop! What color would you make some of the boxes that hold the wands? What about the box Mr. Ollivander is holding?

Every witch or wizard's wand is different. The core of Harry's wand is made with a tail feather from a phoenix. That phoenix was Fawkes, Dumbledore's own animal companion. Fawkes gave a feather to just one other wand—Voldemort's—creating a pairing that would help lead to his eventual downfall.

HARRY POTTER

LORD VOLDEMORT

ALBUS DUMBLEDORE
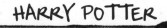

HERMIONE GRANGER

RON WEASLEY

LUNA LOVEGOOD

What would be in your wand? Why?
Write about it below.

_____

_____

_____

_____

_____

_____

_____

_____

_____

Did you know? Actor Richard
Harris, who played Dumbledore
in the first two films, originally
thought that Fawkes was a real
bird. Fawkes was played by an
animatronic in the movies!

LIBRARY

The Hogwarts Library houses books on everything imaginable, including titles like *Hogwarts: A History*, *Goshawk's Guide to Herbology*, and even a book that screams until it is shut. (We don't recommend opening that one.)

What book is Hermione studying from? Using your foil colors, decorate some of the books inside the library! You can decorate Hermione's scarf and tie too.

It is in a book that Hermione, Harry, and Ron discover that Nicolas Flamel was the creator of the Sorcerer's Stone and that Hermione learned what a Basilisk is. Think about your favorite book. What is it? Why is it your favorite? Write your answers below!

_____

_____

_____

_____

_____

_____

_____

_____

_____

_____

THE MONSTER BOOK OF MONSTERS

Of course, not everything at Hogwarts is as it seems. *The Monster Book of Monsters* is an example of that! Hagrid assigns this book to his Care of Magical Creatures students in their third year. Yes, it does contain loads of important information about Hippogriffs, Centaurs, and dragons. But it also bites!

If you were a student in Hagrid's class, you'd learn to carefully stroke the book's spine so it falls open without biting or chasing you.

SCHOOL RULES

During Harry's first year at Hogwarts, he, Ron, and Hermione spend a lot of time visiting Hagrid in his hut. Sometimes, they even sneak out to visit Hagrid after hours. One time, Draco Malfoy follows to spy on them. Then all four students get in trouble for being out of bed!

HONEYDUKES

Honeydukes is a sweet shop located in the wizarding village of Hogsmeade. It has everything a student can dream of: No-Melt Ice Cream, Bertie Bott's Every Flavor Beans, Chocolate Frogs, and so much more! All the sweets are colorful— and dare we say—delicious.

Decorate Honeydukes with your foil. What colors are the Chocolate Frogs? What about the different jars of sweets in the shop?

Of course, Honeydukes isn't the only place where Hogwarts students can find sweets. On their way to Hogwarts, aboard the Hogwarts Express, they can order a variety of goodies from the Trolley Witch.

What is your favorite sweet? Is it crunchy or chewy? Chocolate or fruit-flavored? Whatever you like, write about it!

_____

_____

_____

_____

_____

_____

_____

_____

_____

THE THREE BROOMSTICKS

At the Three Broomsticks, students, Hogwarts staff, and residents of Hogsmeade can order an assortment of wizarding drinks including Butterbeer. Butterbeer is a sweet, delicious drink popular with Hogwarts students.

Finish drawing the Butterbeer in Harry's hand. Don't forget to color it in!

YULE BALL

In Harry's fourth year, Hogwarts hosts a dance called the Yule Ball as part of the Triwizard Tournament. All students who are able to attend wear special fancy robes for the occasion. Using your foil colors, decorate the dress robes that the students wore to the Yule Ball! What color is Hermione's dress? What about Viktor Krum's cape?

THE SWORD OF GRYFFINDOR

The Sword of Gryffindor originally belonged to Hogwarts founder Godric Gryffindor. But now it can be used by any Gryffindor in need, like Harry Potter and Neville Longbottom.

THE TALES OF BEEDLE THE BARD

This book belonged to Albus Dumbledore and was handed down to Hermione Granger after his death.

SCABBERS

The Weasley family rat, Scabbers, was passed down to Ron from his older brothers.

At the Yule Ball, Ron wears
hand-me-down robes that look and
smell like they belonged to his great-aunt Tessie.

Do you have anything that was handed down
from someone else? Perhaps a piece of clothing,
or maybe an important family heirloom?
Write your answer below!

_____

_____

_____

_____

_____

_____

_____

_____

_____

_____

MISCHIEF

Fred and George Weasley are known for their jokes—both at Hogwarts and at home. One of their most talented displays of mischief was a huge fireworks show at Hogwarts. Some of these fireworks made different color swirls, and some were even made to look like dragons!

Using your foils, color in the Weasley twins' fireworks! What color are the small sparkles? What about the big explosions?

Of course, not everyone is a fan of Fred and George's antics. Just ask Mrs. Weasley. She's not afraid to speak her mind—like when she sent Ron a Howler in his second year!

Have you ever gotten in trouble for something you did? Perhaps you didn't do a school assignment, or maybe you flew your family's magical flying car? Write your answer below!

_____

_____

_____

_____

_____

_____

_____

_____

_____

_____

_____

_____

In Harry's third year, Fred and George gift him the Marauder's Map. It's a special magical item that shows the whereabouts of anyone on Hogwarts grounds.

Who do you think is lurking where? Is Hermione in the library? Is Hagrid by his hut? It's your map, so you get to choose! But don't forget to add their footprints to the map!

CHARMS
Classroom

Way to TRANSFIGURATION

PEEVES
LURK
HERE

M A D

HOUSE CUP

Every year the students of Hogwarts compete in the House Cup tournament. They can gain or lose points for their house depending on their behavior and achievements. In Harry's first year, Gryffindor almost lost to Slytherin. But a surprise student helped them take the lead . . . Neville Longbottom was awarded ten points for bravery when he stood up to his friends.

Standing up to your friends is important, especially if you're defending what you know is right. Have you ever been in that situation? Or could you imagine what you'd do? Write about it below!

_____

_____

_____

_____

_____

_____

_____

_____

_____

_____

_____

_____

To announce the winner of the House Cup, the Great Hall is decorated in the winning house's colors!

Use your foil to decorate the banners in the Great Hall, showing who you'd like to win the Hogwarts House Cup!

Have you ever won something that was important to you? Or have you been disappointed when you ended up losing a competition? What did you learn from your experience? Think about it, then write your answer below!

_____

_____

_____

_____

_____

_____

_____

_____

_____

_____

_____

Use these foil sheets throughout the book!